**JUNIORS READ PUBLISHING**

An imprint of Juniors Read LLC

# To my Mom
# who wore the slope,
# *sharply!*

Illustrations by *Guy Wolek*

Cover Design by *Luis Pinto*

Graphic Design and Layout by *Russ Atkinson*

Creative Consultants: *Mindy, Olivia, Vivian, Miriam, and Isaiah Anderson*

Library of Congress Control Number: 2019937425
ISBN: 978-0-9990162-2-0
1 3 5 7 9 10 8 6 4 2

First Edition

Printed in China

VISIT

www.juniorsread.com

# TEN AFROS UP ON TOP

I am Annie.

Izzie, that's me!

'Zinga, we're three!

by Donnie Mustardseed

"Izzie, that's me!
I have big hair!
I like to count
Hairstyles to wear!"

"I am Annie!
And so I fear
There is no style
For me to wear!"

9

"It is not true
Just what you say!
It's just not true.
There is no way!

"There up on top,
  With your big hair,
  Here is a style
  For you to wear!"

11

"Now count one puff
Right up on top!
Here is a style
For you to rock!
So, do you think
This one you'll wear?"

13

"Oh, dear! I think
Not for my hair!
I like this style.
Yes, it is true!
But no, this style,
It will not do!"

"A style on top
For you to rock!
Count one, two mohawk
Styles on top!
So, do you think
This one you'll wear?"

"Oh, dear! I think
Not for my hair!
I like this style.
Yes, it is true!
But no, this style,
It will not do!"

"Now one, two, three
   Knots up on top
   Are bantu styles
   That you can rock!
   So, do you think
   This one you'll wear?"

18

"Oh, dear! I think
Not for my hair!
I like this style.
Yes, it is true!
But no, this style,
It will not do!"

19

"So four twist hairstyles
   Up on top!
   Count one, two, three, four
   Twists then stop!
   So, do you think
   This one you'll wear?"

"Oh, dear! I think
Not for my hair!
I like this style.
Yes, it is true!
But no, this style,
It will not do!"

21

"Now five loc hairstyles
Up on top.
Call hair locks *locs*
When locked on top!
Where? Up on top.
There! Up on top.
Count one, two, three,
Four, five then stop.
So, do you think
This one you'll wear?"

"Oh, dear! I think
Not for my hair!
I like this style.
Yes, it is true!
But no, this style,
It will not do!"

23

"Six high-tops, low-tops,
Slopes on top!
One, two, three,
Four, five, six to rock!
Flattops to wear
Made from big hair.
So, do you think
This one you'll wear?"

24

"Oh, dear! I think
Not for my hair!
I like this style.
Yes, it is true!
But no, this style,
It will not do!"

25

"Count seven updos
Up on top.
Now one, two, three,
Four, five—don't stop!
Six, seven here
Made from big hair.
So, do you think
This one you'll wear?"

"Oh, dear! I think
Not for my hair!
I like this style.
Yes, it is true!
But no, this style,
It will not do!"

27

"Now count eight braid
Styles up on top.
So one, two, three,
Four, five to rock!
Six, seven, eight
All from big hair!
So, do you think
This one you'll wear?"

"Oh, dear! I think
Not for my hair!
I like this style.
Yes, it is true!
But no, this style,
It will not do!"

29

"And nine cornrow styles
Up on top!
Count one, two, three,
Four, five—don't stop!
Six, seven, eight,
Nine styles of hair!
So, do you think
This one you'll wear?"

"Oh, dear! I think
Not for my hair!
I like this style.
Yes, it is true!
But no, this style,
It will not do!"

31

"There are ten afros
Up on top.
Where? Up on top.
There! Up on top.
There are ten afros
Up on top.
And when I count
I just can't stop."

32

"Count one, two, three, four, five, and six.
Seven, eight, nine, and ten—that's it!

Shout one, two, three, four, five, and six.
Seven, eight, nine, and ten—that's it!

Fast one, two, three, four, five, and six.
Seven, eight, nine, and ten—that's it!

Slow 1, 2, 3, 4, 5, and 6.
7, 8, 9, and 10—that's it!

Go one, two, three, four, five, and six.
Seven, eight, nine, and ten—that's it!"

"So one, two, three, four, five, and six.
Seven, eight, nine, and ten—that's it?"

35

"See to count
  Is easy to do.
The more you count,
The more it's true!

36

"Look! Ten afros
Made from big hair
That you can wear
From here to there.
So, do you think
This one you'll wear?"

"Oh, dear! I think
Not for my hair!
I like this style.
Yes, it is true!
But no, this style,
It will not do!"

"There are no styles
For me to wear!
There are no styles
For my big hair!
There are no styles
For me to rock
For my big hair
Right up on top!"

"So those ten styles
  Are not for you!
  But there is one
  That just might do!
  This one right here,
  I like a lot.
  Not of the ten,
  But worth a shot!"

42

"So, do you think
This one you'll wear?
These double puffs
Made from big hair!
Some double puffs,
Like me and you.

Now I wear one . . ."

44

"I wear one, too!

"Right up on top,
From my big hair,
This is a style
That I can wear!
Some double puffs,
Like me and you.
These double puffs—
Yes, they will do!"

47

"We style and profile
Up on top!
Let's count the styles
Of hair to rock.
Yes, one, two, three,
Four, five, and six.
Seven, eight, nine,
And ten—that's it!"

"So miles and miles
Of styles of hair
For me to wear
Made from big hair.
We're pleased to count
These styles to wear!
There, up on top!
All styles of hair!"

49

"Now she has big hair!
I do, too!
What style to wear?
What do we choose?
Some locs that lock?
A puff on top?
Mohawks so tall?
Cornrows that flop?
Or bantu knots?
Or square flattops?
Or round afros
That we can rock?
Or some updos
Made from big hair?
Or twists and braids
That we can wear?
So many styles
Made from big hair!
So many styles
That we can wear!"

"But of these styles,
I choose to wear
These double puffs
For my big hair!"

52

"So of these styles,
From here to there,
Which hairstyle will
**You** choose to wear?"

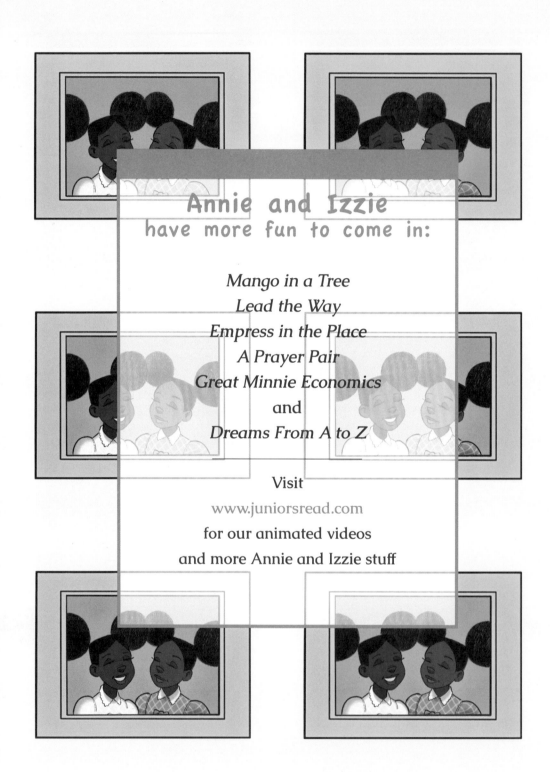

Annie and Izzie
have more fun to come in:

*Mango in a Tree*
*Lead the Way*
*Empress in the Place*
*A Prayer Pair*
*Great Minnie Economics*
and
*Dreams From A to Z*

Visit

www.juniorsread.com

for our animated videos
and more Annie and Izzie stuff